The Spy on Third Base

by Matt Christopher

Illustrated by George Ulrich

SPRINGBOARD
B·O·O·K·S
®

Little, Brown and Company
Boston   Toronto   London

To Daren Krupa

First Paperback Edition

The characters and events in this book are fictitious. Any simi-
larity to real persons, living or dead, is coincidental and not in-
tended by the author.

Library of Congress Cataloging-in-Publication Data
Christopher, Matt.
    The spy on third base.

    (A Springboard book)
    Summary: A third baseman is sick with anxiety about whether
or not to help his team by using his knack for knowing where
the batter is going to hit the ball.
    1. Baseball — Fiction.
I. Ulrich, George, ill.
II. Title.
PZ7.C458Sp   1988   [E]   88-8914
    ISBN 0-316-13996-3 (hc)
    ISBN 0-316-14008-2 (pb)

Springboard books and design is a registered trademark
of Little, Brown and Company (Inc.)

HC: 10 9 8 7 6 5 4 3 2
PB: 10 9 8 7 6 5 4 3 2

MAR

Published simultaneously in Canada
by Little, Brown & Company (Canada) Limited

Printed in the United States of America

The Spy on Third Base

1

He's going to bunt.

T.V. Adams, the Peach Street Mudders' third baseman, studied the Green Dragons' batter, Dirk Farman. Dirk was holding his bat a little lower than usual, and he was leaning forward. T.V. was *sure* he was going to bunt.

It was the bottom of the first inning. Dale Emerson, the leadoff man, was on second base after he had hit a double off Zero Ford.

Bunting wouldn't be the greatest idea right

now, T.V. thought. Not with a man on second base and no outs. But the decision was up to the coach. And, apparently, the Green Dragons' coach had given the batter the bunt sign. It was meant to surprise the Mudders' infield, and it might have if T.V. hadn't figured out the batter's move.

T.V. considered yelling over to first baseman Turtleneck Jones to watch for a bunt. But that would only warn the Dragons' coach and he might change his sign. T.V. decided to keep silent.

T.V. stepped up to the baseline. He was short and stocky, but fast. He ran in a few more steps as Zero steamed in the pitch. T.V.'s heart leaped as he saw Dirk lower his bat and lay a perfect bunt down the third-base line!

T.V. was on it like a dog on a bone. He scooped it up, saw Dale break for third base, then head back for second. But Dale was too late. T.V. snapped the ball to second baseman

Chuck Philips, and Chuck tagged him out.

"Nice going, T.V.!" a fan shouted from the bleachers near him.

"Thanks," T.V. murmured, more to himself than out loud.

Greg Barnes, the Dragons' center fielder, was up next. T.V. watched him carefully. The Dragons wore light-green, white-trimmed uniforms, and Greg's was clean as a whistle.

After Zero blazed in two inside, knee-high pitches, T.V. had him pegged. "Keep them up around his chin, Zero," he said softly.

Zero winked at him, letting T.V. know that he had gotten the message, then threw three straight pitches up close to Greg's chin. The last pitch would have been a ball, but Greg swung at all three and struck out.

"That-a-way-to-go, Zee!" T.V. cried, smacking his bare fist into the pocket of his glove.

Cleanup hitter Eddie Kolski was up next.

Eddie was a right-handed batter, and right-handed batters usually pull the ball to left field. But T.V. remembered that Eddie hit the ball to right field most of the time during batting practice.

"Alfie!" he yelled to Alfie Maples, the Mudders' right fielder. "Play closer to the foul line!"

Alfie took two steps toward the right-field foul line.

"More!" T.V. yelled.

Alfie didn't move.

Eddie connected with the next pitch and drove it within ten feet of the right-field foul line for a triple, scoring Dirk.

"I told you!" T.V. shouted, disgusted.

Alfie didn't respond, as if he hadn't heard him. But T.V. was sure that he had. Alfie had snatched up a blade of grass and was chewing it.

Then Andy Jackson came to bat and

slammed a grass-cutting grounder halfway between T.V. and the bag. T.V. dived for it, gloved it, then whipped it to first.

Too high! The ball sailed over Turtleneck's head. Eddie scored. Andy went to second base, and T.V. was chalked up with an error.

Peach Street Mudders 0, Green Dragons 2.

He was sick.

2

"Guess you didn't predict that bad throw, did you, T.V.?" a voice said as T.V. headed back to his position.

T.V. glanced toward the bleachers and saw that the speaker was the same fan who had yelled to him earlier. He was tall and husky and wore a red sweatshirt. A short kid with thick glasses was sitting next to him.

T.V. didn't answer him. He couldn't take the time to talk to a fan right now, no matter whose side he was on.

Cush Boochie popped a fly to Bus Mercer at shortstop, ending the bottom of the first inning.

"You're up, T.V.," said Coach Russ Parker as he headed for the third-base coaching box. "Let's get on."

T.V. got his bat and stepped into the batter's box. He wished he could predict what right-hander Bucky Neal would pitch to him, but he couldn't. Not this first time, anyway.

"Strike!" the ump boomed as Bucky steamed in a knee-high pitch.

Bucky's second pitch was almost in the same spot. *Crack!* T.V. corked it to right center field for a double.

He felt better. The hit made up for that wild throw.

Chuck Philips flied out to left field. Then Alfie sparked up the team by smashing a ground-ball single through second base, scoring T.V. Bus walked. And Rudy Calhoun,

10

with three balls and a strike, blasted a triple to the left field fence.

The fans loved it.

Watching them closely from second base, T.V. had figured out almost exactly where the batters were going to hit the ball. He hadn't figured on Bus getting a walk — that was the pitcher's doing, not the batter's — but his guesses about Chuck's and Alfie's hits were right on the button.

Guesses? No. He studied the way they stood at the plate and the way they swung at the pitches, and he knew. He didn't have to guess.

Both Zero and Barry popped out, ending the half-inning. But the Mudders had chalked up three runs to go into the lead, 3 to 2.

The Green Dragons picked up a run during their turn at bat, then held the Mudders scoreless in the top of the third.

Eddie Kolski led off in the bottom of the third and connected with a triple. It landed in almost exactly the same spot where he had hit his first three-bagger. Again Alfie had ignored T.V.'s advice to play close to the foul line.

What do I have to do to make you believe me? T.V. felt like shouting at him.

Andy Jackson drove a sharp liner over Chuck's head, a hit that T.V. hadn't counted on. He predicted Cush Boochie's ground ball to short, which was an out. But he failed to read Beans Malone's buntlike hit toward third base correctly. Both were hits he never could have predicted, even if he'd been able to read a crystal ball.

"Closer to second, Chuck!" T.V. cried to his friend at second base as the Green Dragons' first baseman, Lefty Cash, stepped up to the plate. "Stay in center, José!" he yelled to the center fielder, José Mendez.

This time T.V.'s prediction was almost perfect. Lefty slammed a pitch directly at José but slightly over his head. José ran back, reached for the ball, had it for a moment, then dropped it!

"Oh, no!" T.V. moaned.

Bucky Neal doubled, scoring two runs.

The inning ended with the Dragons leading, 6 to 3.

"Hey, T.V.," the man in the red sweatshirt said as T.V. headed for the dugout. "You can really read those batters."

The boy with the glasses, who was eating a hotdog now, smiled. "Yeah. What are you, a spy?" he said, then chuckled.

3

A *spy*? T.V. wondered what he was talking about.

Then he realized the kid must have meant that T.V. seemed to know a lot about the Green Dragon batters.

He gave the sod a hard kick as he headed for the dugout. Spy! That kid made it sound as though T.V. had done something sneaky.

"What's the matter?" asked Mickey Stanner, the team's scorekeeper, as T.V. sat down beside him.

T.V. wedged his glove between them. "A guy in the stands called me a spy."

Mickey chuckled. "So, what's so bad about that? I wouldn't mind being compared to James Bond."

T.V. had to smile. "Yeah, I guess there are worse things than being a spy."

"Yeah, like having to move," Mickey grumbled.

T.V.'s eyes followed Chuck Philips as he stepped up to the plate. "What did you say, Mickey?"

"Nothing. Just that I'm moving away." Mickey pushed his sunglasses up on his nose.

"Oh? Have you told Coach Parker?"

"Not yet," Mickey said.

"Better tell him," T.V. suggested. "We can't play ball without a scorekeeper. Especially a good one like you."

Mickey grinned. Few guys paid any attention to the scorekeeper. He just did his job and hardly ever said anything. The coach might have a tough time finding a replacement for him, T.V. thought.

T.V. turned back to the game and saw Alfie strike out. Then Bus walked, and Rudy flied out, ending the top half of the fourth inning.

Neither team got a runner on base again until the last inning when, with two outs, Chuck drew a walk.

"Keep it going!" Coach Parker cried from the third-base coaching box.

T.V. glanced at the scoreboard on top of the fence in left field. It was still Mudders 3, Dragons 6. I wonder what it would have been if I hadn't figured out where the Dragons were going to hit the ball, T.V. thought. Probably Mudders 3, Dragons 12.

But the Mudders had to get hits, too, he told himself. Without hits you don't get runs.

He could read those Dragons like a book. They could still be beaten. He was sure of it.

It was up to him.

He put on his helmet, picked up his bat, and stepped to the on-deck circle. José was leading off.

"Come on, José!" T.V. called to him. "Belt it!"

José grounded out to short. Then T.V. stepped to the plate.

"Where you going to hit it, T.V.?" the short kid in the bleachers yelled at him. "Over the fence? Ha! Ha!"

Oh, pipe down! T.V. wanted to say to him.

He took three balls and a strike, then flied out to center field.

"Tough luck, T.V.!" cried the man in the red sweatshirt as T.V. walked sadly back to the dugout.

Chuck drew another walk, Alfie singled, and the Peach Street Mudders began to roll. The bases were loaded when Zero came to the plate. The lefty already had a single to his credit. T.V. felt sure that Zero had done his share for the day.

He began to reach for his glove when *crack!* came the solid sound of bat meeting ball, and T.V. saw the white pill soaring to deep right field! His heart soared, too, as the ball sailed over the fence for a home run!

The Mudders fans went crazy. Zero was the last kid on earth anyone would dream would hit a grand slammer!

"Keep it going, Barry!" T.V. shouted, as Barry McGee came to bat.

He didn't. He flied out. Mudders 7, Dragons 6.

The Dragons came to bat for their last chance, and T.V. studied the leadoff batter, Lefty Cash. Lefty had already gotten a single,

and had struck out his second time up. But T.V. didn't think that Lefty was a weak hitter because he batted eighth in the lineup. He could still be dangerous.

"Play deep, you guys!" he yelled to José and Alfie.

José moved back, but Alfie didn't.

He resents my telling him where to play, T.V. thought, a little hurt.

Zero stepped on the mound, got the sign from Rudy, then pitched. *Smack!* Lefty met the ball head on, driving it to deep right field. It missed being fair by inches!

"Back up, will you, Alfie?" T.V. shouted again.

This time Alfie moved back closer to the fence.

Smack! Another long drive to right field! This one was fair!

Alfie, his back against the fence, jumped and caught it.

"Good catch, Alfie!" T.V. shouted.

The fans gave Alfie a lusty cheer.

One out.

T.V. had Barry play close to the foul line on Bucky Neal, and Bucky nailed one directly at him for the second out. Then Dale grounded out, and the game was over. Mudders 7, Dragons 6.

T.V. leaped with joy as he ran in toward the dugout.

"Nice game, you guys!" he cried, slapping Chuck on the back and then Alfie. "Great catch, man! Like a big leaguer!"

Alfie's eyes narrowed. "You the coach or something?" he said, his face straight as a ruler.

"Yeah," Chuck cut in, eyeing T.V. as if he'd done something dirty. "You act as if you're the only one with brains. The only one who counts."

4

T.V. stared at them.

He couldn't believe it! His best friends —
Chuck and Alfie — saying those awful things?
Had he sounded so bad?

"I didn't mean . . ." he started, but stopped
short. He didn't know what to say. He didn't
think it would make any difference to them.
They had made up their minds, and nothing
he could say would change them.

Heck, he thought. I didn't mean to *boss*

them. I wanted to *help* them. Help the *team.* And I did. Don't they realize that?

He looked around and saw that they were already heading off the field. Almost always the three of them would walk home together. Now, suddenly, a barrier had come up between them, just because he had wanted to help. Maybe being a spy wasn't such a great idea after all, he told himself.

"T.V.!" someone called to him. It was Coach Parker.

"Nice work out there," the coach said, smiling. "You figured out those Green Dragon players pretty well."

T.V. shrugged. "Yeah. But I guess the guys aren't that keen about it," he replied. He was glad, though, that the coach had noticed it. He hadn't thought about that.

"Don't worry about it, T.V. Maybe one or two aren't, but most of them are." The coach paused, thinking. "Why don't you give them more of a chance the next time? Let them use their own judgment. If you see they can't do as well, then use yours."

T.V. grinned. "Okay."

"You never know," Coach Parker said. "You might wind up being a great coach someday."

T.V. laughed. "Oh, sure!" he said. "Well, I've got to go."

He started to head toward the gate.

"Just a minute," the coach called to him. T.V. turned. "A reporter, Mel Thompson, was asking me a lot of questions about you. He noticed your ability to predict where the batters were going to hit and was really impressed. He wondered how you do it."

T.V. laughed and shook his head. "I just study the batters, that's all. I don't *always* guess right."

"Maybe not. But most of the time you do."

T.V. felt nervous. He'd never thought

guessing the batters would have attracted that much attention, especially from a newspaper reporter.

"He might still be around," Coach Parker said, glancing behind him. "If you'd like to meet him —"

"No! I mean, I can't," T.V. said, starting to edge toward the exit. "I promised my parents I'd come home right after the game."

The coach waved. "Okay. Take care."

T.V. left the park and headed for home, thinking about the dumb excuse he'd given to the coach. His parents probably didn't even know he *had* a game. His mother always seemed to be too busy, and his father had never played a sport in his life, unless you counted horseshoe pitching.

As he had suspected, his parents were surprised to see him in his uniform when he got home.

"Well, how did you make out?" his mother asked.

"We won," T.V. said, collapsing into a chair.

"Congratulations," Mrs. Adams replied. "How about celebrating with some dinner?"

T.V. was hungry enough to eat a horse, but not exactly in the mood for celebrating.

"Guess what?" Mr. Adams said to T.V. when he came to breakfast the next morning. "You made the news."

T.V.'s appetite disappeared. He had forgotten about the reporter at yesterday's game.

His father picked up the *Morning Herald.* "Listen to this:'Theodore Vernon Adams, the Peach Street Mudders' sensational third baseman, has more up his sleeve than a good throwing arm. In a tense game against the Green Dragons, yesterday, he predicted almost *exactly* where the batter was going to hit more than 90 percent of the time. What is this boy wonder's secret? Is he psychic?'"

5

"*Psychic!* Me? Is he nuts?" T.V. cried. He started to run out of the room.

"Hold it, hold it!" his father called to him. "What are you angry about? That's *good* news, not bad."

"Right," said Mrs. Adams. "We always knew you were smart, but we had no idea you had such a special talent."

"Mom . . ."

"I'm just teasing you. Come back here and tell us all about it."

T.V. inhaled a deep breath, let it out, and sat back down. He was halfway through explaining what the article was about when the phone rang. His mother answered it.

"T.V., it's for you," she said.

He took the receiver from her. "Yes?"

"Hey, man!" said a male voice. "See this morning's paper? It says you're psychic!"

A cold streak shot up T.V.'s spine. "Who is this?" he demanded.

"Don't try to use your 'powers' in the game against the Stockades, or you'll be sorry. And you know it!"

Click! The caller hung up.

T.V. returned to the table, his heart pounding.

"Who was that?" his father asked, peeking around the edge of the paper.

T.V. avoided his eyes. "Some kid . . . calling about the article."

"Sounds like your fame is spreading quickly," Mr. Adams said.

"Lucky me," T.V. mumbled.

Mr. Adams laid the paper aside and patted T.V.'s hand. "Don't worry, son. This too shall pass. Pretty soon you'll be just a regular guy again."

Not soon enough, T.V. thought. But in the meantime, he promised himself, he would try to put the phone call out of his mind.

That afternoon T.V. got out his swimming trunks and went to the park pool. It was sunny and hot and he was sure a good swim would make him feel better.

When he got there, some of the guys looked familiar. He recognized two from the Stockade Bulls baseball team. The short, husky one was Chet Barker, the Bulls' catcher. The tall, skinny one was Stick Jolly, the Bulls' third baseman.

"Look who's here! T.V. Adams, the great mind-reader!" Chet yelled. He was standing on the diving board, ready to dive off. Stick

was sitting on the edge of the pool, his wet black hair matted down.

T.V. blushed. Oh, no, he thought. Not that again.

"See you made the headlines!" Stick's high-pitched voice came across the pool. "Wow! A psychic! You might be on TV, T.V.! Hah!"

T.V. glared at him.

Stick and Chet laughed.

"Don't let those goons get to you," someone said from behind T.V.

T.V. whirled around and found himself facing Alfie. Chuck stood next to him, shuffling his feet.

"We saw the article about you," Alfie said. He seemed nervous. "And Chuck and I were talking."

"We're sorry about yesterday," Chuck said. His eyes were red from swimming underwater. "We acted like jerks."

T.V. grinned. He felt as though a block of ice had melted inside him.

32

"Coming in?" Alfie asked. "The water's great."

"Yeah," T.V. said. "I'll go change, and . . ."

Just then Stick walked up to them, a crooked smile on his face. "How do you do it, T.V.? What kind of power have you got?"

T.V. tried to keep his cool. "I haven't got any power," he said firmly. "I just study the batters, that's all. Anybody could do the same thing."

The crooked smile broadened. "Well, look, pal. Don't try to study us when we play you guys on Thursday."

Stick's threat sounded familiar, but T.V. was sure that Stick wasn't the one who had called. Not with that high voice.

"He's right!" Chet Barker yelled, springing up and down on the edge of the diving board. "It'll never work on us! We're the Bulls, man!"

Then he dove, making a complete turn in the air before straightening out and hitting the water, fingertips first.

6

The day was gray in more ways than one as T.V. Adams waited for his turn to bat. There wasn't a blue patch in the whole sky, as if the sun were having a day off. And T.V., gloomy as the day, had made up his mind he wasn't going to do any "spying" in this game against the Stockade Bulls. He'd been threatened too many times and the butt of too many jokes since the game against the Green Dragons.

And just a few moments ago someone in the crowd had shouted at him, "What's he going to do, T.V.? Hit or strike out?"

The person was referring to José Mendez, who was batting now. It was the top of the first inning. There was one out, and Bus was on first base. He had smashed a single through the pitcher's box. I don't know and I don't care, T.V. wanted to say to the fan, but he kept his thoughts to himself.

José drilled a line drive directly at the first baseman. Bus started to run, then bolted back to tag up. Ted Jackson, the Stockades' first baseman, beat him to it. Three outs.

"Okay, T.V.!" yelled that same voice again as the teams exchanged sides. "Now's your chance to see what you can do!"

T.V. tried to ignore the heckler, but it was hard to ignore a voice like that. It sounded as if it were coming out of a bull horn.

T.V. watched leadoff man Jim Hance tap

the end of his bat against the plate, then stand with it about six inches off his shoulder. After two sharp swings, T.V. had a good idea where Jim might hit the ball — if Jim hit it at all — but he kept his prediction to himself. He wasn't going to get involved with that sort of stuff again.

Sparrow Fisher, on the mound for the Mudders, threw the next two pitches outside. Then Jim popped out to short left field, exactly where T.V. had thought he would. And Phil Klines grounded out to the shortstop.

Then Ted Jackson singled, and cleanup hitter Adzie Healy stepped up to the plate. After Sparrow's second pitch and Adzie's first swing, T.V. had a strong hunch that Adzie was going to hit the ball to right center field.

Sparrow blazed in the next pitch and, as T.V. had predicted, Adzie slammed it directly to right center field for a triple, scoring Ted.

But that was it. Catcher Chet Barker — the

kid T.V. and Chuck had seen at the pool —
flied out to left.

The Mudders couldn't do anything until
the top of the fourth inning, when Chuck
doubled to left center field and scored on Turtleneck's single. Then Rudy knocked Turtleneck in with a big triple to deep right field
but died on third base when nobody could
hit to score him.

The Bulls had scored three times in the
bottom of the second inning. And now, in the
bottom of the fourth, they were going great
guns again. Ralph Healy, Adzie's brother, had
started it off with a ground double to right
field. And Adzie ended it with a home run
over the left field fence.

Mudders 2, Stockades 8.

T.V. had predicted another long ball rock-
eting off Adzie's bat because of Adzie's strong
swing. But, in spite of the wise remarks from
some of the fans, he preferred to keep his calls

to himself. Maybe they'd forget about him and keep their mouths shut.

"You haven't said a word to any of us the whole time," Alfie said as he trotted off the field with T.V. "You're not keeping mum because of what Chuck and I said to you after that first game, are you? We said we were sorry."

"No," said T.V. "It's not that. I've just changed my mind, that's all."

Alfie gave him a long look and didn't say any more.

The game ended with the Stockade Bulls winning 10 to 2.

That night T.V. received a phone call — a very short call — from a familiar voice: "Thanks, pal."

7

T.V.'s hand shook as he put down the receiver. He still didn't know who it was, but it didn't make much difference. He had never felt more humiliated in his life.

Suddenly, he began to feel mixed emotions. Was he right or wrong to let the fans and the Stockade Bulls needle him into keeping quiet about his predictions?

Maybe, if he had spied on the Stockade batters and told his teammates how to play them, the score might have been a lot different, 4 to 2, or 3 to 2, say.

He felt guilty. He had let his teammates down. Darn! he thought. I can't win! No matter what I do!

It was only eight-thirty when he said goodnight to his parents and went to bed. He didn't want to stay up and think about that call and the game any longer.

But sleep didn't come easily. Now his mind churned with questions about his having special "powers." Those two guys in the stands and that newspaper article had sure started something.

The thoughts were even stronger in his mind the next day. He was sitting on the front porch, facing the street, when he said to himself, "Maybe I really *am* psychic. Everybody seems to think so, even that reporter. Maybe I'm a *freak*!"

He hadn't realized that he was talking out

loud until he said "freak!" He turned around to see if anyone had heard him, but he was alone.

"Oh, boy, T.V. thought. I've gone bananas!

His stomach began to feel woozy and he went inside. He lay down on the living room sofa and soon fell asleep. He dreamed that some stranger whose face he couldn't see was chasing him. He screamed and screamed.

Somebody shook him awake. He opened his eyes and stared into his mother's worried face.

"T.V.! You were having a bad dream!" she whispered. "How do you feel, dear?"

"My stomach . . ." he started to say, then wished he hadn't. He knew what she would say now.

"I'm going to have your father take you to Doctor Erickson."

Just what he had figured.

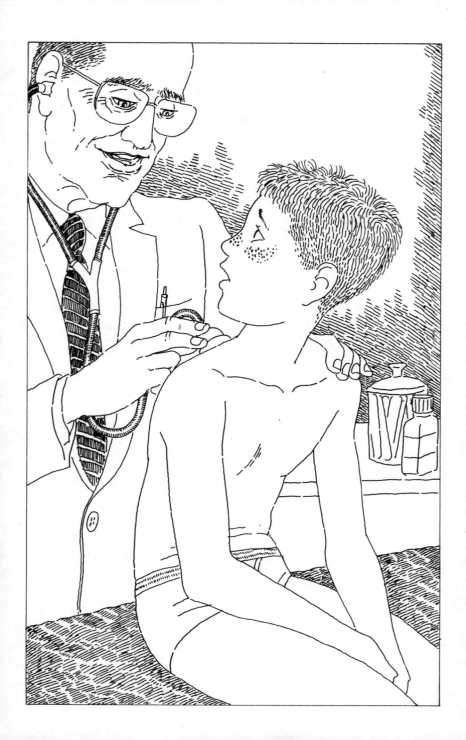

Within an hour, T.V. was on the doctor's cushioned table, shaking like a nervous puppy. What if the doctor found something wrong with him? What if he really *was* different from everyone else?

8

The doctor set aside his stethoscope and smiled. "Worried about something, Theodore?" he asked. "Like not getting hits in your baseball games, maybe?"

T.V. shrugged. "No."

Dr. Erickson put his hands on T.V.'s knees and looked him straight in the eyes. "Get any ribbing from people — from the fans — about that reporter's little joke? You know, about those 'powers' you have?"

T.V. stared at him in surprise. I guess every-one in town — maybe in the whole state — has read that column! he thought.

"I think that's your problem, T.V.," the doctor said. "You're worried too much about what people are saying. And all that worrying is making your stomach hurt. It happens to a lot of us." He smiled again and patted T.V. gently on the shoulder. "You're perfectly fine. Put your shirt on."

T.V. left the doctor's office feeling like a million bucks. He was normal!

In the car going back home, Mr. Adams said, "Look, T.V., if baseball is bothering you this much, maybe you ought to give it up and try something else. Like horseshoes, maybe."

T.V. grinned. "I'll think about it," he said.

He liked pitching horseshoes. But he wouldn't trade baseball for anything. He still loved it, no matter what.

They were driving by the public swimming

pool when T.V. spotted his friend Chuck Philips.

"Dad!" he cried. "Will you let me off here?"

His father slowed the car down. "Then Doctor Erickson was right? You were just worried about that article?"

T.V. nodded. "That and the phone calls."

"From whom?"

T.V. shrugged. "I don't know. I guess that proves I'm not psychic, huh?" he said with a smile.

Mr. Adams laughed as he pulled the car over. Then he put his arm around T.V.'s shoulders and got serious. "Don't worry about them. Anybody trying to scare you with phone calls hasn't got the guts to meet you face to face. Think about that."

T.V. looked at him. His father's words tumbled around in his mind until they settled down and made sense.

"Thanks, Dad," he said. "See you later!"

T.V. hopped out of the car, ran across the walk to the pool, and tapped Chuck on the shoulder.

Chuck spun around. "Oh, hi," he greeted T.V. "I thought you were sick."

"I was . . . in the head, mostly," said T.V. "Who's our next game with?"

Chuck thought a moment. "The Bearcats," he said.

"They got a good team?"

"Let's see," said Chuck, squinching his eyebrows. "I think they've split so far. Won one and lost one."

"When do we play them?"

"Next Tuesday." Chuck looked steadily at T.V. "Think you'll be well enough to play by then?"

T.V. grinned. "I *know* I will," he said.

The evening before the game against the Bearcats, T.V. got a phone call.

"Adams, don't do any spying in tomorrow's game, or you'll be sorry. And you know it!" a male's voice said before hanging up.

It was the same voice as before.

T.V. laughed. "Yeah? We'll see about that, buster!" he said and hung up, too.

9

T.V. ate a hearty breakfast the morning of the game against the Bearcats.

"Well, how about that?" exclaimed his mother. "I guess you've recovered from what ailed you."

T.V. wiped his mouth with a napkin. "I feel a lot better, Mom," he admitted.

"Well enough to play baseball?"

"Definitely!" he said.

But he didn't say anything about spying on

the opposing batters. Right now he wasn't sure whether he was going to or not. Maybe his father was right, and maybe he wasn't, maybe a guy who made threats over the phone didn't have enough guts to meet him face to face.

T.V. thought about the man in the red sweatshirt who always sat near the dugout. He looked strong enough to rip a phone book in two. But why would he make threatening phone calls? It didn't make sense.

Late that afternoon, T.V. put on his uniform, got his shoes and glove, and headed for the ball park. On the way he met Mickey Stanner, the Mudder's scorekeeper.

"You going to spy like you did in the game against the Green Dragons?" Mickey asked.

"I don't know," T.V. said truthfully. He changed the subject before Mickey could say anything more about it. "Have you told the coach that you're moving?"

"Yeah. But he still hasn't found another kid who wants the job."

T.V. shrugged. "I'm sure he will soon."

"Who cares anyway?" Mickey said. Then he stomped off, leaving a baffled T.V. behind him.

The teams took their infield practice. Then, promptly at five-thirty, the game started. The Bearcats had first bats.

T.V. watched the leadoff batter closely as he tapped the end of his bat against the plate a couple of times, then faced the Mudders' pitcher, Zero Ford. Sparrow was supposed to pitch, but he was home with a cold.

He's going to drive one to left field, T.V. predicted as he watched the batter.

And that's just what Horace Robb, the batter, did. He powdered Zero's third pitch to left field, directly at Barry McGee, for the first out.

51

T.V. watched Jack Walker, the Cats' second batter, closely, too, and predicted that he was going to drive a long ball to left field also. After two straight strikes, Jack slammed two out there. Both went foul. Then Zero struck him out.

"Aren't you spying this game, T.V.? Or are you going to keep it all to yourself?"

T.V. glanced at the bleachers and saw the same two guys he had seen at the other games — the short kid with glasses and the man in the red sweatshirt. The man smiled and waved.

T.V. returned the wave and turned his attention back to the game.

Suddenly it broke wide open as Boots Finkle walked, Luke Bonelle doubled to left center, and Jim Jakes singled, scoring two runs. Then Rusty Carson flied out to center for the third out.

The Mudders got a fat zero at their turn

at bat, and the Cats came back and earned three more. 5 to nothing.

Oh, wow! T.V. thought. *This is turning into a disaster!*

Chuck led off in the bottom of the second with a homer that dazzled the crowd. But that was all the Cats allowed the Mudders. They came to bat in the third, leading 5 to 1.

"They're beating the tail off you guys, T.V.," the kid with the glasses said. "Lucky for that homer, or it could have been a shutout."

T.V. felt his heart pound, but he kept his tongue.

10

Jim Jakes led off in the top of the third for the Bearcats and slammed a sharp single over shortstop Bus Mercer's head. The hit brought a round of applause from the Cats fans and a ripple of laughter from the kid with the thick glasses.

"Keep it going, you Cats!" the kid said. "Lay it on good and heavy . . . like peanut butter on a slice of bread!"

Out to get my goat, T.V. thought. Well,

he's got it. But this is as far as it goes. Dad's right. Whoever threatened me on the phone did it just to scare me. He doesn't have the guts to say it to my face.

I bet it was that kid, he thought. It had to be someone who was at every game, and it couldn't be any of the Mudders. He doubted it was the man in the red sweatshirt — he seemed friendly.

T.V. turned to look at the kid in the stands and met his eyes squarely. Then T.V. smiled, looked away, and began to concentrate on the next batter. He had had enough. He was going to spy again . . . starting now!

He watched Rusty Carson swinging his bat, and thought: *he's going to hit it to me!*

And Rusty did. T.V. caught the sharp, bouncing grounder, pegged it to second, and Chuck relayed it to first for a double play!

"Close in, José!" he shouted to the center fielder.

José moved in closer and only had to take two steps forward when Drew Zellar popped him a fly.

Zero led off the bottom of the third with a single, starting off a hot inning that netted the Mudders two runs. Both were on a triple that T.V. had cracked out to right center field.

No one scored again until the top of the sixth, when Rusty Carson homered over the left-field fence. T.V. had warned Barry to play deep on him, but Barry was no giraffe. He could never have caught that long, hard fly.

Bearcats 6, Mudders 3.

"Our last chance, T.V.," Chuck said as T.V. stepped up to the plate.

T.V. took a called strike, then streaked a single through the infield. *Bring me in, Chuck!* he pleaded silently at third base.

Chuck popped out.

Then Turtleneck walked and Alfie doubled, bringing the Mudders one run closer.

"Get a hit, Rudy!" T.V. cried when he reached the dugout. "Don't let them die there."

Rudy struck out. "Oh, no!" T.V. moaned. It looked hopeless.

Two outs, and Zero came to bat. T.V. was sick. He could tell Zero was going to strike out. He just *knew* it.

"Watch it, you guys!" he shouted, kiddingly, to the Bearcats outfielders. "This guy's going to belt it out of the lot!"

He might as well have a little fun, he thought.

"Oh, no, he isn't," a voice spoke up beside him. "And you know it!"

T.V. straightened as if someone had jabbed a rod against his back. *And you know it.* That voice! Why hadn't he recognized it before? He had heard it not only here in the dugout, *but also on the phone.*

He turned and stared into Mickey Stanner's eyes. "You!" he cried. "You're the one who's been calling me!"

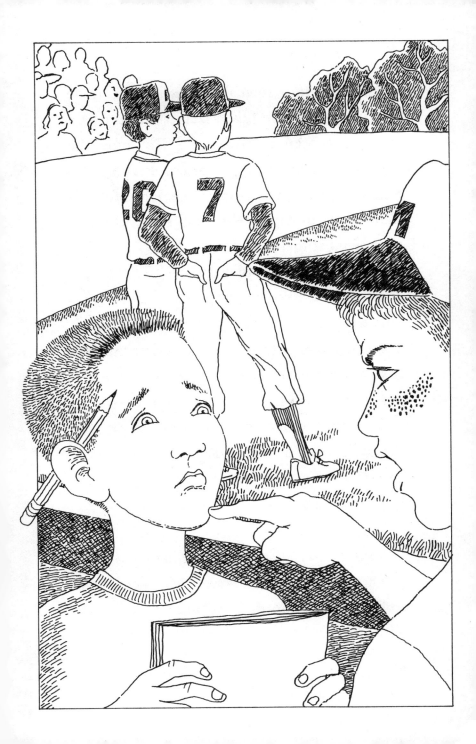

Mickey's face turned red as a beet. "No! Not me. I . . ." He faltered and stared down at the scorebook in his hand. "Why not?" he admitted finally. "I'm just a scorekeeper. Nobody pays any attention to me, except when they want to know who bats next. Or how many hits somebody got."

"But why did you pick on *me*?" T.V. asked. "I thought we were friends."

"Some friend," Mickey whined. "You don't even care that I'm moving. All you care about is your dumb spying!"

Crack!

T.V. turned in time to see Zero powder the ball out to deep right field! It was going . . . going . . . and it went over the fence for a three-run homer!

The fans went wild.

So did T.V. He couldn't believe it.

The whole Peach Street Mudders team spilled out of the dugout and greeted Zero with high fives as he crossed the plate.

It was over. Bearcats 6, Peach Street Mudders 7.

T.V. looked for Mickey in the confusion. He finally found him, standing by himself.

"Hey, I'm sorry if I ignored you, Mickey. I've had a lot on my mind lately."

Mickey looked down, embarrassed. "I'm sorry about the calls, too."

"Just promise me you won't pull anything like that in your new town. Okay?" T.V. said.

"I promise!" Mickey cried. Then they shook on it.

T.V. saw two familiar faces approaching him, and he ran forward to greet them.

"T.V., did I hear you predict Zero's grand-slammer?" the man in the red sweatshirt asked.

T.V. laughed. "I was just kidding. Then *he* fooled *me*!"

The man said, "I'm Mel Thompson. I'm the one who wrote that article about you."

T.V.'s mouth dropped open. So this was the guy who had caused him so much trouble!

"And I'm James Boles," the kid with the glasses said.

"Glad to meet both of you," T.V. said. Then he turned to the boy. He felt guilty about suspecting him earlier. "James, you come to all the games. How'd you like to be the Peach Street Mudders' official scorekeeper?"

James Boles' eyes bulged behind his thick lenses. "Me?"

"Yes, you."

"Wow! Sure!" James cried. Then he frowned. "But you have a scorekeeper."

"Not for long," T.V. said.

"Are you predicting this, or are you sure about it?" Mel Thompson asked, grinning.

T.V. grinned back. "I'm one hundred percent sure about it!" he said.